BOXES, BOXES, EVERYWHERE!

Written by
Crystal Bowman

Illustrated by
Jane Schettle

Zonder**kidz**

The Children's Group of ZondervanPublishingHouse

Boxes, boxes,
EVERYWHERE!

In the hallway,
on the stair.

Boxes, boxes,
big and small.
I don't like boxes,
not at all!

Glasses

What's in the boxes?

LOOK and SEE-

My shoes, my toys,
my chimpanzee.

My pillow, books,
and rocking chair,
My very favorite teddy bear.

We're moving somewhere else today.
I like my house.
I want to stay.

Good-bye, big truck—

ZOOM, ZOOM,

Good-bye, my house,
good-bye, my room.

Mama stoops to kiss my hand.
She tells me,

**JESUS
UNDERSTANDS**

He left his house
and his room too,
So he could go
to someplace new.

Then Mama takes me for a ride.
We find a house
and go inside.

Boxes, boxes,

EVERYWHERE!

In the hallway,
on the stair.

Towels

Books

Toys

Blanke

What's in the boxes?

LOOK and SEE-

My shoes, my toys,
my chimpanzee!

My pillow, books,
and rocking chair,
My very favorite teddy bear!

I like my house,
I want to stay.
Thank you, Jesus, for this day.

Good-bye, big truck—

ZOOM, ZOOM,

Hello, my house,
hello, my room.

ZOOM,

Boxes, boxes
big and small,
I like boxes,

I LIKE THEM ALL!

Mom's Moment

Our children often feel uneasy in the midst of changes, like packing and moving, until they discover something that hasn't changed, like the presence of their favorite toys and family members. As moms, we often face changes that make us feel uneasy, until we discover that God hasn't changed. He promises that he is with us always, and in the midst of change, he remains the same. We can rest securely in the comfort of that truth.

Text copyright © 2000 by Crystal Bowman
Illustrations copyright © 2000 by Jane Schettle
Printed in China
Art Direction and Design by Michelle Lenger
Requests for information should be addressed to:
Zonderkidz, Grand Rapids, MI 49530